Winter Fun

LET'S GO ICE-SKATING!

By Jasper Bix

Gareth Stevens
PUBLISHING

Please visit our website, www.garethstevens.com. For a free color catalog of all our high-quality books, call toll free 1-800-542-2595 or fax 1-877-542-2596.

Library of Congress Cataloging-in-Publication Data

Bix, Jasper.
Let's go ice-skating! / Jasper Bix.
pages cm. — (Winter fun)
Includes index.
ISBN 978-1-4824-3755-3 (pbk.)
ISBN 978-1-4824-3756-0 (6 pack)
ISBN 978-1-4824-3757-7 (library binding)
1. Skating Juvenile literature. I. Title. II. Title: Let us go ice-skating!
GV849.B57 2016
796.91—dc23

2015023049

First Edition

Published in 2016 by
Gareth Stevens Publishing
111 East 14th Street, Suite 349
New York, NY 10003

Editor: Ryan Nagelhout
Designer: Sarah Liddell

Photo credits: Cover, pp. 1, 7, 15, 19 LWA/The Image Bank/Getty Images; cover, pp. 1, 9, 19, 24 (helmet on all) ronstik/Shutterstock.com; p. 5 Tyler Olson/Shutterstock.com; p. 11 Africa Studio/Shutterstock.com; pp. 13, 24 (blade) kuzsvetlaya/Shutterstock.com; p. 15 (helmet) BlueOrange Studio/Shutterstock.com; pp. 17, 21, 23, l i g h t p o e t/Shutterstock.com.

Printed in the United States of America

CPSIA compliance information: Batch #CW16GS: For further information contact Gareth Stevens, New York, New York at 1-800-542-2595.

Contents

On the Ice 4
Heads Up! 8
On Blades 12
Gliding Away 20
Words to Know 24
Index. 24

Winter can be fun.
Let's go ice-skating!

Make sure
you dress warm.
The ice is very cold.

Wear a helmet.
This keeps you safe.

Make sure
your skates fit!
Tie them up tight.

Be careful with
your skate blades.
They are sharp!

Learning to skate
takes time.
Try not to fall!

Try to walk
in your skates.
Start with short steps.

Push your feet
forward on the ice.
This is called gliding.

Glide back and forth
on each foot.
This is skating!

Next you learn
how to stop!

Words to Know

blade

helmet

Index

blades 12

gliding 18, 20

helmet 8

skates 10, 12, 16